BEFORE I BECAME A BUTTERFLY

Before I Became A Butterfly
Edited & Compiled by
Czarina Datiles

Paperback Edition

First published in India in 2023 by

Inkfeathers Publishing
Vivek Vihar, New Delhi 110095
www.inkfeathers.com

ISBN 978-81-19483-45-7

BEFORE I BECAME A BUTTERFLY

Edited & Compiled by

Czarina Datiles

Inkfeathers Publishing

www.inkfeathers.com

Disclaimer

The anthology "Before I Became A Butterfly" is a collection of 8 short stories and 32 poems written by 25 authors who belong to different parts of the world.

Unless otherwise indicated, all the names, characters, objects, businesses, places, events, incidents—whether physical/non-physical, real/unreal, tangible/ intangible in whatsoever description used in this book are either the product of the author's imagination or used in a fictitious manner. Any resemblance to actual persons, objects, entities, living or dead, or actual events is purely coincidental.

The contents published in this book are solely owned by their respective authors and are in no way intended to hurt anyone's religious, political, spiritual, brand, personal or fanatic beliefs and/or faith, whatsoever. In case, any sort of plagiarism is detected in the contents within this anthology or in case of any complaints, grievances, or objections, neither the anthology editor nor the publisher is to be held responsible.

For Didas, thank you for fostering my imagination and wit.

For Mamis, thank you for your endless wisdom.

Curated with the writings of

*Kelly Keyes, Olympuz, Pia, Leah Legan, Abigail Alcala,
Mia Grace Davis, Marissa Wilfahrt, Czarina Datiles,
Claire Casapao, Saraswathy, Pawan Kumar, Kashish Lewis,
Anannya Tiwary, Kai Jennings, Pavika Pandey,
Aarushi Agarwal, Rhythmi Rosa S., Khushi Mahla,
Divvya Gupta, Ashlesha Misra, Jothika Pandiarajan,
Binta Elsa Biju, Sanaa Shaikh, Jasmeen Bagga, BB*

Contents

Acknowledgements

No one really reads the acknowledgements; I know I usually don't. But for those who are reading it, this is for you.

To Didas and Mamis, to whom I dedicate this anthology, thank you for the eighteen years of love and support you endlessly gave me. Know that I write not just for myself but for you, too. I want to make you proud. I want to ensure the investment of time, energy, and money you put into me was worth it. Mahal ko kayong dalawa.

To Meiko and Muymuy, the reason behind my early maturation and grey strands of hair, thank you for being the best brothers I could ever have. When this is published, I'll treat you both to boba drinks.

To Mama and Momo, the strong-as-a-bull Valentina and William, thank you for your selfless sacrifice and the love you put into my raising. Mahal ko rin kayong dalawa. Yes, you can now tell the whole of Gatchalian.

Thank you to Anna, Kayla, and Sophia, who have been my most amazing friends for twelve years (and counting!). I'm so grateful to you three for being there when I needed you most. I love you all endlessly.

Thank you also to the teachers at my elementary/middle school, St. Therese Academy. To Mr. Sperrazzo, Mrs. Ledford, Mrs. Balistreri, Ms. Zora, Mr. Peterson, and Mrs. Peterson—thank you for being the best supporters of my writings. Thank you to the Academy of Our Lady of Peace for being the space where I could fully blossom. To Mrs. McDaniel, who was the first teacher to read my most vulnerable writings, and to Mrs. Hillier for her guidance in polishing them—you both are the reason I had the courage to publish this. I'm also incredibly grateful to Mr. Gonzalez for helping me build my confidence as a person and to Coach Higgs for allowing me to use that confidence to flourish as a leader.

Finally, to Isabel, my literal partner-in-crime. This is for us. Here's to what we were, what we've gone through, and what we have become. I love you so much!

Editor's Note

In elementary school, we learned the process of how a caterpillar becomes a butterfly. It begins with the caterpillar forming a chrysalis around itself, during which metamorphosis occurs, breaking down body tissue to prepare for the growth of wings. Once it has fully become an adult, the changed caterpillar breaks out of its shell and emerges as a new entity: a butterfly, becoming a symbol of change and love to everyone.

Similarly, we have all undergone our own transformations. Whether that be a child's physical and mental maturation into an adult or the emotional and spiritual changes we go through at various points in our lives, we are constantly renewing ourselves. As for myself, the past three years have been a whirlwind of emotions, ranging from hurt, jealousy, loneliness, and anguish. At the lowest point in my life, I found comfort in the company of words. I realized how raw yet empowering we become when we express ourselves in the privacy of paper and pen. Writing has become a source of comfort for me, and like many of the authors who have contributed to this collection, it has allowed me to become someone I can be proud of.

The stories and poems included in this anthology reflect our shared experience of growth. As we know, growth is not linear but a process of successes and setbacks. As you begin this collection, enter with an open heart and a strong mind like a caterpillar ready for change. Some stories can be difficult to read as they deal with trauma, loss, and heartache. But know this is a safe space where hard but important experiences are told. Allow our words to touch your hearts, maybe even tear them a little so that the lessons learned can inspire renewal within them. And once you've finished, we hope our stories have encouraged you to return to life with a new spirit.

We hope that you will become a butterfly just like us.

The saying from the Greek philosopher, Heraclitus, goes, "The only constant thing in life is change." So, embrace it, yearn for it, and seek it. Life is about reinventing ourselves. Learn from what you've lost, take what you have, and make something beautiful out of it.

With much love,

Czarina Datiles

Meet the Editor

Czarina Datiles is an eighteen-year-old Filipino writer and poet from San Diego, California. A national medalist in the 2023 Scholastic Art and Writing Awards, her works have been recognized by The New York Times and published in The Weight Journal and Synchronized Chaos. Although words are her passion, she is pursuing a university degree in Global Health, where she seeks to travel to remote places around the world and help those in need. She loves rainy days, fantasy novels, good company, and boba drinks.

Flying Higher Than the Wind

Abigail Alcala

They're small with so much life. They're clean and so sweet. They don't always know the path and where they're going next, but that doesn't stop them.

Butterflies bloom like flowers. They might be small, but they are so brave. They once crawled, but now they fly and live like they couldn't fly tomorrow. From day to night, they soar with passion and courage, knowing obstacles will be in their way. There will be wind and birds and people trying to stop them from getting to their destination. But the butterflies know that there are people who are jealous of them and who wish they would fall down the deep, dark hole just like Alice.

The caterpillar becomes the butterfly for a reason. Not because the caterpillar thinks it's ugly or unworthy but because it grows with the wind blowing it away. The more it grows, the more the wind's jealousy intensifies, and the more the wind wants to see it fail. That won't stop the caterpillar; it'll keep on getting up because it knows who it used to be and grew for a reason: to fly like nothing can touch it, to fly like there's no tomorrow.

It flies like the butterfly I am.

The Dark

Marissa Wilfahrt

The dark,

It frightens most

Not only for causing the lack of sight

But because it leaves one defenseless

It strips one's control from them and leaves them in the shadows

Of their own thought

Nothing crowding one's eyesight

Nothing turns one's head when the thought of reality
begins to seep in

Nothing illuminating a path lined by those meant to guide others

Nothing but darkness

It holds a certain irresistible allure, nonetheless

For it is a mystery, and it is solitude

The cold attacking one at their most valuable state

But all there is to do is to live in the numbness,

To let it consume you and feel the vastness of feeling nothing at all,

To surrender to the dark's temptation,

And to sit with the companionship of one's own mind

In wait for the moon's bright arrival

Funny Little Thing Called Anxiety

BB

funny little thing that is anxiety

comes and goes like a pandemic

in a pandemic full of pity

you'll find it in streets with car trunks full

frozen embarrassment in a malice city

look under your sheets, under your feet

a rotten piece of meat, something you can't beat

there you will meet

this funny little thing called anxiety

it, with blue lips and a few flips,

having tea with your insecurity

look under the rug of the future; there it sits

wearing a cloak of invisibility

It is still testing the horses in our heads,

bidding on the way, we'll sweat

it doesn't spill our secrets

it is our secret

a barrel rolling down the last thread

it comes with a company

a silent disco of panic attacks

drinks from the hot and cold punch bowls

drips down our backs

bangs on the doors of your pulse

in fear, you run in your converse

you run faster

but it always comes first

with a touch of popularity

in this distressed city

There lives a funny little thing called anxiety.

Sea Salt and Open Eyes

Pia

The older I get,
the less tangible
my emotions become.

First, it was fear,
but now it's that anxiety
I can't quite name,
that mark resting on my heart
that burns,
like sea salt to open eyes.

And still, I burn and
hold the brand it left me—
the image of the world that
owns me.

But now it's that heaviness,
that cloud overhead that never dissipates,
and that sadness like soft rain
falling on these lonely nights.
That kind.
I'm crying, and so's the sky with me.

The Girl in Pyjamas

BB

This is a story about a girl in pyjamas

cranky little thing in her pool

she's surrounded by the nauseous scent of

alcohol-painted nails, she curls up in a ball

it's Fall here in mid-October

cheeks dryer than all the maple leaves

all her friends are lying on the grass

with their hand-holding in the car's

backseat: she sits in the middle, playing music

for them, it feels just like a movie where they kiss

in the end.

girl in pyjamas is a wonderland in her own

acts mental sitting with one numbed leg

in a baseball t-shirt, screaming at her phone

she can't escape this facade of a room

coincidentally, it's also painted blue

a blue coffee mug sits idle like her

she doesn't know all the pretty words,

all the pretty boys or the pretty girls

she doesn't know how to feel love
only to feel the pain that goes above
her throat
her hair
her skin that's fair
jealous all the time
a girl that only bites
a girl that laughs at her jokes
a girl that chokes on her words
a girl that is afraid of her world
the girl in pyjamas is a messy girl
egocentric mind stalker
emotionless prick
she plays all of her tricks
then shuts herself in a locker
calls herself an alien in a spaceship
a girl so bad at relationships
is it a fault of her own

that she's all alone?

I Want to Be Myself

Jasmeen Bagga

I want to untie the hundred social skills I learnt for the
sake of fitting in,
I want to unmask the thousands of veils I clothe every day,
I want to skin down every layer of unknown wrapped around
my body
until there is nothing left but me, me and me.
I want to scrap off the millions of faces until all that's left
are the two tired eyes,
which I truly recognise.

I want to read Milk and Honey for the thousandth time,
I want to be myself, no one but myself this time,
I don't want to tear off my jeans
or hide my books
while I smile and greet with my face painted red and pink,
I don't want to
mould me up and about
shadowing the span between my thighs,
the curves of my spine,
the width of my waist,
burrowing my nails deep into my skin,

while I uproot my apple-white stretch marks
as I have done in the past.

I want to wear them around like well-built tree roots,
staying grounded in the unique beauty that is myself,
I want to turn toward the library while others make their way
through the clubs and retreats,
I want to stand in front of a goddamn mirror.

I want to be myself again, no one but myself this time
because
what I saw, others turned a blind eye to,
what I heard; others turned deaf to.
I am a no-one,
a story without narration,
a rotted apple in a dozen,
a branch with no stem.

unattached, left out, not a member—
No—I never did fit in.

I wanna untie the hundreds of social skills I learnt
for the sake of fitting in.

Stalker

Saraswathy

Gowri stirred in her sleep. Her eyes opened, and she turned towards the alarm on her bedside table. Her roommate was fast asleep.

Was it dawn already?

No, the alarm wasn't ringing. Outside, the night was still dark. She pulled up the blanket, turned sideways, and tried to go back to sleep. Then she heard it— a little rap on the window of her room. Jolted awake, she sat in bed and looked out the window. A man stood outside; his silhouette visible in the dimly lit hostel compound. His features were obscured. Gowri froze with fear and inhaled sharply. The man then disappeared beneath the windowsill.

"Hey, wake up." Gowri climbed down from her bed and shook her roommate awake.

"What…" Her roommate opened her eyes groggily.

"I saw a man near the window." Scared, Gowri went behind her roommate Reena's bed. Reena sprang up too, and together; they stood there for a minute.

"Should we go and check?" Reena asked.

"Where? In the middle of the night?"

"Should we wake up the warden?" Reena offered. "How did he even get in? With the watchman, gate, and fence?"

"I don't want to go out." Gowri shivered. The way the man stood there had stirred fear in her. Eventually, she switched the lights on. "Maybe he will go away. Let us wait."

Under the lights, the two saw a note stuck in the net of the window, sticking halfway inside.

Gowri giggled nervously. "A note? For us?"

They waited there, anticipating any movement outside the windowsill. When nothing stirred, Gowri plucked up the courage and pulled out the note, reading, let me in, baby… let me in. Her face crumpled in disgust, feeling nauseous.

"Some crazy man." she muttered, crumpling the note with indignation and throwing it in the dustbin.

"How can he…" Reena scowled. "The nerve of some people."

The girls switched off the lights and went back to bed. They didn't sleep until dawn.

*****

"But how can he come in?"

Gowri and Reena were discussing last night's intrusion during a period break. The other girls in their class were also left aghast when told what had occurred.

Gowri carefully pulled out the next hour's lecture notebook. "Never mind. Maybe he won't come again."

"Imbecile," Reena spat. "But think about it, Gowri. He couldn't have come through the main gate or the fenced wall."

"Could he have come through the teacher's quarters?" Gowri asked. The teacher's quarters were in the same compound, separated by a small, locked gate and a medium-height wall. "But how did he get into that compound?"

The lecturer entered the class a moment later, and the two stopped the discussion. They agreed to write off the incident as a bad dream. Still, a few days later, as Reena was turning in and Gowri was writing on her desk, a small whistle distracted Gowri from her studies. She turned towards the window, surprised.

The man returned and was standing near the window.

Gowri gasped with fear and indignation. She didn't know what to do. The man whistled again, demanding her attention. She sat there, trembling. Her mouth was dry. The man lit a torch, pointing it downwards. She saw his unzipped pants, his genitals in full view.

Shocked, Gowri wanted to call out and say something as the man. But instead, she pulled back her chair and switched on all the lights, awakening Reena.

"What?"

The man waved and ducked under the windowsill. Gowri told Reena what happened, and she wondered whether they should wake the warden. But she was too scared to open the room door.

"Let us tell her tomorrow morning," Reena advised her.

*****

"What do you mean?" The warden, an elderly lady, was dubious. "A man outside your window? But this hostel has so much security."

"We saw him," Reena and Gowri said in unison. They were hesitant to tell her about his display.

"He can't come from outside," the warden explained. "There is no way he climbed in from the top of the fence or the gate. He could have used the teacher's compound…." The warden frowned. "Maybe he is someone who knows the premises or has access to that compound somehow. Either way, I will also alert the watchman and ask around at the teachers' quarters if they see anyone. Should he come again, give me a call."

"In the middle of the night?" asked Reena.

"Yes. He can't come in here." The warden was firm in thwarting the miscreant, allowing Gowri and Reena to leave reassured.

Later in the evening, Reena came into their room with a parcel— looking like a book— and a few letters.

"Did you order any books?" She asked. "There is one for you and a letter as well." Reena handed Gowri the parcel and letter before leaving to deliver letters to the other girls on the floor.

Gowri opened the letter first. It was from her younger sister, which included trivia and some inquiries about her studies from her parents. When Reena returned to their room, Gowri opened the parcel. It was covered with brown paper and without a postal stamp. Only her name, room number, and hostel name were written in crude handwriting. There was no "from" address. Puzzled, she took out a book and gasped in shock.

Reena looked at her. The book was written by "Anonymous." It was porn, hardcore porn. Gowri was used to reading Mills and Boon, but this was disgusting and offensive. She threw it down with annoyance and anger.

"It's that man," she said.

Reena picked up the book. "Do you want to take it to the warden?"

"Burn the bloody book." Gowri was seething. The madman won't leave her alone.

Reena quietly picked it up and went to the warden. Ten minutes later, the warden came into the room.

"Did you see anyone following you around?" She asked.

"No, ma'am." Gowri was close to tears.

"I will keep this in safe custody," the warden said, gesturing to the book. "Someone must have dropped it in the big postbox. He knows the hostel well." She turned to Reena. "Should you see anyone, let me know."

Somehow, Gowri wasn't reassured. The stalker was closing in on her.

*****

It was a Friday afternoon, and Gowri and Reena had just finished a long lunch break. Gowri had a practical class and stood outside the classroom, taking out her previous class reports and records.

"Oh no! I left my record back in the hostel room."

"The teacher will ask for it," her classmate said. "Maybe recheck your bag."

Gowri went through it once more but still couldn't find it. "Listen, I will run along and get it while you get your records corrected. Just tell her I will be back." Quickly, she dropped her bag, took the room key, and ran back to the hostel.

When she arrived, Gowri took out the record and ran back. The lane from the hostel to the college was deserted in the afternoon, and in her hurry to reach her class in time, she didn't hear the noise of a bike coming behind her. She turned back only when she heard the noise at a very close proximity. She recognized it was the man from the window. The helmet was hiding his face.

The bike stopped, and two rough hands grabbed her, turning her outward, facing away from the bike. One closed over her face and mouth roughly, blinding and choking her. The other groped her hurriedly and savagely. She tried to push away the hands and free herself from panic. But he continued to grope her as much as he could for fear of someone catching him. After two minutes, he pushed her face to the ground, left her, and sped away on his bike before she could get up.

Shaken, Gowri dragged herself to the school nurse, who applied Neosporin to her wounds, patching the bruises on her hand, legs, and face. One of her cheeks was badly bruised by a metallic talisman on the groper's wrist, secured with a thread. They were two small threads, partly red and partly black, like a patchwork.

"Couldn't you be more careful? At your age, you shouldn't be slipping or falling. You could have been seriously injured." The nurse was taking a syringe out to give a tetanus injection.

Gowri couldn't tell the nurse the truth. She had told the nurse that she slipped and fell on the road. The nurse informed her teacher and classmates, and she got sick leave for a half day.

In her room, Gowri tried to sleep, feeling violated and ashamed of herself. She recalled how the man's fingers had touched her, how they had moved over her. Her skin still burned at the memory of his unwelcome and intrusive touch. Telling this to others was like reliving the ordeal. It was humiliating. Gowri couldn't help but wonder why, being the victim, she was ashamed when it was he who had assaulted her.

She didn't share her ordeal with anyone. She quietly ate the painkiller the college nurse gave her and tried to close her eyes. She felt defeated, bone tired, and did not know how to save herself from this stalker.

*****

She was running frantically, calling out to others. A rabid bull was chasing her, and she was running through alleys, past houses and buildings. But the bull didn't stop, and neither could she. Nobody could help her.

Suddenly, she came to a blind alley. She had nowhere to go. She turned back towards the bull. The bull was closing in on her. She took it by its horns and pushed it back. The bull staggered, and she pushed again with more force. The bull retreated and ran back.

She stood there sweating.

She was safe now; she was free.

Gowri woke up drenched in sweat. It was clear to her what she must do to get rid of the stalker. All the strength she needed was within her. There was no question her inner self couldn't answer, no problem she couldn't solve. Gowri no longer felt helpless or alone.

Gowri felt the heat of the furnace as she pummelled at the cylindrical model with a hammer. It was a sample that needed to be altered into a square using the furnace. The model was nowhere near a square. The smithy was part of their practical classes.

The lab attender, a middle-aged man whom everyone called Chetta (meaning brother like bhaiya in Hindi), used to help them out. He came near Gowri and said, "Give me the hammer."

She turned obediently and gave it to him.

Looking into his face, she saw his expression, which displayed superiority and a sense of possession. Baffled, she thought he felt high-handed about his pummelling skills or strength. But as she watched him lift the hammer and smash it down, she noticed a talisman with black and red threads.

He was the stalker, she realized.

As she stared at the talisman, the attendee took notice of her tension and looked into her eyes. Gowri discovered that he knew she knew.

It was now or never. She had to confront him, or else he would continue harassing her as if she were his property. She could not do it by saying he was her stalker. He would likely just say no; it would be her word against his. Though no one would doubt her, everyone would try to silence her, trying to play safe. He would then walk free, thinking what he did was acceptable. And if he were a permanent employee, the authorities wouldn't be able to do much. The union would back him.

But he did not scare Gowri. Not anymore. Quickly, she raised her foot, hooked her ankle into his, and pushed him off balance with all her strength. He rolled down into the dull red heat of the open electric furnace. The hammer fell with a thud and loud clatter.

He let out a scream.

The students in the class turned towards him. Gowri screamed, exhilaration pulsing through her.

"Help!"

Maybe she was cruel. But so was he.

People were taking him out and calling for an ambulance. Gowri didn't look back. She ran out, covering her face. People thought she was upset at the accident. A few girls ran after her to console her.

But Gowri didn't need any comfort. She felt calm; she felt strong.

In life, one had to fight one's own battles since no one else would. There wasn't a problem that the inner self couldn't solve. This realization stayed with Gowri for all her life.

Bluff

Aarushi Agarwal

All the cuts, all the lies,

the hidden truths

that made you cry

I know it's hard

it's just not fair

for the times to leave you

in such despair

It can be hard

It can be tough

It can be just like

a game of bluff.

You hide the truth

you don't let them know

You do cry

you just don't show.

Times can be hard

It can be tough

But you need to know

you just can't give up.

All the cuts
that you made,
it's not done
It's not your mistake.
These marks will last
all your life
They'll remind you of
the harsh times
that you had to face,
that you are facing now
Uplift your soul
Heal the dark hole
made by the grief
in your heart
All the pain
that tore you apart.
You need to know
You need to feel
the happiness
this time for real
It can be hard

It can be tough
You need to stop playing
this game of bluff.

Will I Let Demise Win?

Pavika Pandey

I wandered into the woods at night

As I heard a bird sing to me,

In its ominous tone,

As I speak through my poetry.

They whispered to me their melancholy,

"Can you listen to me?

My heart is craving harmony."

The somber melody spun through the air like a gossamer dream

As a spiral of wrath filled my eyes with green.

Sadness reigned the world at that hour

While walking down with elegance from its royalty.

I bowed my head, piously cursed.

Inside I writhed, I moaned, I tore open my soul.

The winds supported me, made me groan in agony,

A hollowness surrounded me from within

As death echoed and throbbed in my veins.

Every breath seemed like the last,

Every second seemed to pass.

My heart, a stained glass of pain,

My mind, a flurry of white noise,

My soul, some disintegrated molecules of black smoke.

And my body, oh my body,

Burns with the agony of the world.

Leave me, oh dear demise,

I'm begging you to leave me.

Don't dare mourn the person I metamorphosed into

For I'm the strongest one alive,

Strong enough to shred you apart.

I cannot rule shackled to this earthly flesh.

Pierce me with darkness, oh demise,

And see me shine like the stars in my eyes.

The throne waits for me in the abyss of the cries,

And in the labyrinth of cries shall I fight demise.

I will rise and let the pain die,

You put me down, but my beloved,

Just like air, I'll rise again

To rule my coven in the skies.

And all left in my wake are the ashes of your expectations.

Now the pain is nothing but a shimmer of dust.

And oh, dear demise, at last, I have won,

As I paint my victory on the canvas of history,

As I clutch my dying heart with all of my might,

I'll paint with my blood till I meet demise.

I'll let go, oh, lord of death, for it is you who has won this bet.

And like a phoenix, again, I will rise from

All the ashes you left me in. For it'll smoke fire when we meet
again.

But till then, you rule while I mend.

Free, I'm Free

Divvya Gupta

We met at the crossroads,

Last time, to cut the node.

I walked away; I wanted to be gone.

My departed feet heard your curse

About how I won't have a purpose from now on,

And the fact that you hope that I drown,

Engulfed by the despairing cyclone.

It would sadden you to know

That I still smile, and my cheer is wonderfully alive,

And how I feel no void,

No pain.

Instead, I'm complete and sane.

Wow! How godly this is, the feeling that I say,

As I sit under the tree,

Just me and the breeze:

I feel free!

While I sit here,

Waiting for the stars to honour the sky,

And for them to be my spotlight,

To guide and ignite me,

And even if I've to walk alone, I know I can make it my own,

Artistically,

Maybe messily,

But bravely.

Cause I hear the whispers of the breeze,

Loud and clear,

"You're free, My Dear!"

And guess what?

I won't leave footprints behind,

I won't let you find me,

Chase me,

Or meet me,

I'll take a leap this time,

A bigger leap,

Away into a place of serene,

To echoes of the breeze,

For a wish to always hear: "I'm Free!"

Desire's Wish

Marissa Wilfahrt

Why must I be apart from you?

I make many a wish each morn

The most profound of which be my need

To feel what you do

That I may be licensed to your present opinion of me

I long to hold you in my arms

To explore the mystery, we call love

To talk and to reminisce

To break down walls

And if the shame of rejection is my worst consequence

Then the prospect of my acceptance

Is more than a worthy risk

A Corner Mail

Pawan Kumar

My Name is Rachit Saini, and I am a student at IIT Kanpur. I was in love with a girl in my college. She was someone who changed my perspective on life, whose presence showed me the true meaning of love. She put truth to the saying, "A girl in your life can change thousands of negative things into positive vibes within you."

We talked about the future, about you and me, but living in Uttar Pradesh was difficult. I knew our parents might not support our love and intercaste marriage. Parents fought and even died for religion and caste, never agreeing to a happy married life. We fought over it, too, and slowly our anger turned into bitterness until we stopped talking. Eventually, she told me it was over.

Since then, I've tried everything to reach out to her, and every time, I failed. So, for the last time, I'll send this email, my final attempt, before we become strangers forever.

Shreya,

I like to think about our memories. It never bothered me if you had been with others. I was sure that our future would always shine with our love and affection for each other. We were happily committed to each other at IIT. I stopped drinking coffee for you and began drinking tea, knowing you loved it so much. I chose my Night recharge pack over a bottle of Coke if it meant extra minutes of talking over the phone with you. Those were the golden moments of our relationship when I saved every penny for us.

I never called anyone, not even my batchmates, who could have helped me in lectures and lab work. Hello Tunes and other mobile services were out of the question, even though it was trendy and cool. I saved every bit just to talk to you because phone calls were our only source of communication. It bridged the gap between us and gave me a reason to live from the start to the end of the day.

My first phone was exclusively for you. Almost all of my monthly expenditure was just phone recharge and nothing else. My first priority was you. Always you.

Shreya, you are the only one I ever desired. I can share anything with you, from books to perfumes, shoes to my Britney Spears playlist. But I couldn't share you with anybody else.

Yes, I was possessive of you. I cancelled my road trip to Banaras because I didn't want to leave you alone. Instead, I accompanied you on your bus to Agra. I knew you were mature enough to travel by yourself. But I left you alone at a party once after one of our arguments, which I still repent for, and I didn't want to do it again.

On that bus ride, I gave you my seat so that you could comfortably sleep. Though let me confess, I smelt your hair while you were leaning against my arm. I knew you wouldn't like it, but I did it anyway. I'm sorry.

Do you remember our first movie date? I took a whole day off because I wanted to create some kind of spell on you, just like Shahrukh Khan did in his Hindi movies. Trust me; I had no intention of touching you. I'm sorry that my arms touched yours in the theatre. That day, you yelled at me, and at that moment, I felt like I meant nothing to you.

Our parents taught us that boys don't cry. But the truth is that boys do cry in private. Whenever I saw you flirting with your fellow batchmates or getting too close to any other guy, I felt empty. I never had the words to express that feeling. But I cried. I cried for you in the boys' hostel washroom, invisible and inaudible to everyone.

I've hurt you many times. I know I wasn't always a perfect person. There are so many things I wish I hadn't done. But I tried to make you happy, to give you surprises each day, from roses to chocolates. I spent hours creating a pickup line for my early morning text before you woke up. I did everything to make you smile.

I love you as my own flesh. I've never needed any female companions to make me feel good. I longed for you and only you.

I'm single and living my life without you. But you still dominate my thoughts. You must have so many important things and people in your life. I hope to be your friend, but I feel like I can't meet your expectations. I want to ask you to come back into my life, but I know it's better to go our separate ways.

Still, don't hesitate to call me if you ever change your opinion. My number is the same.

I hope you find your perfect person soon. But I want you to know that I still think of you, and no one can love you as much as I do.

And before I forget, I want to give you a parting gift, an unpublished book I wrote. I won't meet you, but if you accept it, tell me where I can leave it for you. You may read it, throw it away, or give it to someone else. It's your choice. But I hope that you read it.

Yours truly,
Rachit Saini

Thoughts of our beautiful college time have made me more confident than insecure. I've realized that love teaches you to respect a person, trust your lover, and be there for them when no one else can. I've learned how to make life beautiful with pain. I've understood that life is a gift from God. Life is to forgive others and bring someone joy with your presence.

After four years, this mail remains in my "Drafts Folder." I've never had the courage to click send for my beloved recipient. It reminds me of my immaturity and how I still have much to learn in being humble and respectful towards someone. I still have room to grow.

Without You

Sanaa Shaikh

When I pass by the little ice cream shop on the corner,

When I feel the gentle wind ruffle my hair like you used to,

When I wear the bracelet you carefully crafted for me,

I realize that I still miss you.

When I visited the parks that we frequented,

When I belt out the songs that you listened to all night,

When I read the books that you insisted I do,

I realize how much I still love you.

When I see your smile in an old photograph,

When the ghosts of our late-night conversations come back to haunt me,

When euphoric memories of our past threaten to ruin my present,

I realize that you make up half of me.

The truth is, I'm still learning what it's like

To walk by places that remind me of you,

To rewatch the movies that you cried your heart out to,

And to live with the ache of doing it all without you.

The Spell of the Cabin

Abigail Alcala

I was left in a cabin without food, water, or life. Nobody put me there. I walked in. I walked in with security, confidence, and happiness, but as soon as I came in, I felt the insecurities flow through my veins. Thoughts ran through my head, saying, "Kill me, kill me." I couldn't seem to find a good thought.

Tears as clear as water streamed down my face. I saw everything that was wrong with me. I saw things that haunted my thoughts. I saw them in pictures and mirrors and everything that gave off a reflection of what I really looked like. Growing up, my family told me I was beautiful and said everything I needed to hear, yet I never believed them. I never looked at myself the same. I saw myself differently from everyone around me. I saw myself as fat and ugly, not thin and beautiful. I never saw myself as beautiful as a butterfly. I saw myself as the slimy green caterpillar that nobody thought of.

Would anyone care if I disappeared like the clouds in the night sky? I knew my friends didn't care. They wanted me gone ever since I got there. This spell took over my thoughts and feelings. I never forgot the spell of the cabin.

Mirror Lies

Jothika Pandiarajan

I used to love my mirror
From my childhood
Cause it showed someone pretty

I always wondered
Who's this?
I always liked to stand in front of it

To see what was happening
I was pretty shocked
When I cried

My mirror girl cried, too
When I laughed
My mirror girl did the same

When I felt sad
She, too, looked alike
A twin sister

Born together with me
She only appeared
When I looked into her
But I got to know the truth
I know my mirror lies
When there's no such person

It's only me who's before it
I'm standing
In front of it

It's just a single piece
But reflects all colours
Of our life memories

It's as strong as diamond
It will be multiplied
When broken into pieces

Many faces are shown
When broken
Sometimes I'm like a

Broken piece, too
When I look into it
My broken heart reflects everywhere
I know mirrors lie
So, I enchant myself
Show my happy face in front of it

Surprisingly, I'm pretty again
Many pretty faces are shown, too

Love Without Restraint

Marissa Wilfahrt

Now that the last brick of the final wall is gone,

I may love without restraint.

There is no judgment nor expectation,

And I may ask the questions my mind dares to think.

You answer them.

I never believed people who spoke of somebody who wasn't like
anybody they'd ever met.

I doubted love.

I was weary of its constraints,

But now that the last brick of the final wall is gone,

I may love you free of restraint.

midnight drive

Czarina Datiles

Sometimes I stare out the window,
watching flashing streaks of hopeless dreams
run opposite of me
as the hour hand of twilight
reminds me that it's time to sleep.
I scroll on Instagram instead
because it's better to drown in
insecurities
than lie awake with existential crises
and perpetual gloom.
Yet, when I do,
I fall into the eye of a hurricane,
a sacred place of silence and abandonment
surrounded by spiraling screams
and flying cows.

Despite the calm,

I long for what lies in the gray sky,

the turbulent winds,

the flying cows, the wooden floors

of a broken house

because a still pond always longs for rain,

even if she holds water.

the ripple of a single drop

quenches her unbearable thirst.

At the end of the late-night drive,

I set my phone aside and set my eyes

back on the road with streaks of hopeless dreams

running past me.

I hear my pitiful mantra echo in my head,

the only words that keep me from self-loathing

and existential dread.

I am where I need to be

But is that really the case?

Or is it my own misery and envy

that I can't seem to face?

Space Poets Hope

BB

My hopes fall in a pool of a dense night

the subdued fear and intense shivers

take over my shoulders and tear them apart

clear pearls blanket my spine line

the hopes swim and sink deeper

shade pokes out my iliac crest

I never got the fern leaves tattoo

the pain is just as much as

Austria will never be called the City of Music

with my screech in The Cranberries

today is the sixteenth of trick or treat

I've been tricked more often

bleached more often than the beach

lingered on like a leech

wanting more of Sarah and Mitch

What is Abercrombie and Fitch?

a space poet paints my paintings

mucked pastel across the collar

as my bones pout inside a tin

teeth licking sourness in

feels more than normal

space poet stands by the door

a boombox built-in

my windowpane shakes in the voice of Musgraves

it's too cute to take it to the grave

my brutalized hopes decay

in the space poet's boots

I started walking barefoot

fly away in the galaxy's dust

with Sylvia Plath's bell jar

Austria never seemed so far

Uncertain

Marissa Wilfahrt

Though I yet to know

The destination of my fate

Nor what shall bring it upon me

Death has no hand in life

Death has no hand in marriage

Death has no hand in dance or song

Death has no hand in love

So I shall not succumb so easily to it

As the leaves do

When the wind taps them off their stronghold

I shall not fear Death

As I shall not fear life

One casts immortality, the other some experimental years

Though I yet to know the time

When I shall meet my expiry from Death

Nor what he shall inflict upon me

When the clock enters my hour

I shall be ready for his confrontation

To Breathe Underwater

Kai Jennings

I'm fifteen now, trying my best to be a butterfly and spread my beautiful, colorful wings. The only problem is I don't have any. Even if I did, am I ready to take flight?

Covid started when I was eleven, and my parents enjoyed pissing the government off. They went to parties and walked openly on the streets during the lockdown, maskless. Two days before turning twelve, I got a message from my friend:

Dude, I'm so sorry.

I didn't understand.

Sorry for what? Stealing my chocolate two years ago?

More of the same messages appeared until I asked them what was going on. They told me my parents had been killed by Joel Hatley, a man trapped in India for Covid. At the time, I was crushed. It was difficult to accept. I was called to the police station and didn't understand a word they said to me. The world felt numb, and I was trapped in a heartless life like a genie imprisoned in a lamp.

From there, I was sent to live with my aunt, who stayed on the other side of Mumbai. She never understood how I felt. Not when I started a new school or was paraded around as 'the kid who lost his parents.' A lot of people hated me. Even worse was that they pitied me. A few didn't care, and those few were my friends. They didn't give a shit about what happened to me unless I did.

That was the problem; I never did. I simply zoned it out like I did everything else. I hated thinking about it. Eventually, my aunt noticed. She asked me what was wrong, but I didn't know, so I just shrugged her off. I continued until I was sent to therapy. There, instead of shrugging at my aunt, I shrugged at my therapist. She asked me what I saw on a page of ink splotches, and I shrugged. She asked me what I liked to eat, and I shrugged. She asked me what music I listened to, and I shrugged.

I was diagnosed with manic depression and sent off with pills that I never took. I would just sell them even though I was perfectly fine financially.

At some point, I stopped shrugging. I started thinking. It was hard to think about myself since I hadn't done so in a long time. I had to clean out the cobwebs and dust and oil the gears so that it would start. By that time, I wasn't sad about my parents anymore. I realized they had been terrible people, leaving me alone to get high with strangers in cocktail dresses even when they were alive.

It shouldn't be a surprise that they're dead.

But that wasn't all I felt. I wanted to scream; I wanted to cry; I wanted to destroy. I started drowning in my own feelings. It took years until I learned that I could breathe underwater. So underwater, I lived, trying to be the happiest I could be, trying to be a butterfly.

Californian Skies

Pia

I grew up on
Californian tie-dye skies,
eclipsed by swaying palm trees
that are dancing in time
to the music of bitter waves breaking
on an even colder shore.

I got older and watched the
Devil winds come
and shake trees so hard
they howled with fear,
like coyotes under crescent moons.
I stood looking over harsh cliffsides
to which pebbles try so hard to cling
onto those seaside daggers.

I gazed towards seas of stars,
stolen from the sky
by those city lights—
We wanted them closer than ever.

Still, the sun bleeds into a new day
in some parts of the world,
making those same
tie-dyed skies.

In the Memory Lane…

Binta Elsa Biju

Walking down memory lane,
Mind over brimmed with
Varied emotions and memories of
Hateful and blissful moments.
I picked up a sweet moment
From the valley of the past and
Eagerly long to experience it now.

But I found it fades in the
Relentless storms that cause

Great havoc in my life.

Moving on… my mind stuck at
Another moment in the past.
"Move on; don't get stuck."

I heard a voice that
Murmurs in my heart.
At that moment, I raised
My head and look at the future.
Future didn't give me a
Warm smile, as I had always
Spent my days with 'past and present.'

Hey! I called out.
Future blinked its eyes
As a sweet gesture.
Then I made a promise that
I'd continue my journey-

Looking forward to a
Bright future.

follow the wind

Czarina Datiles

The wind used to be my enemy. It was always so temperamental. One day it was crisp, cold, soothing on the skin, and peaceful for the mind that worried about heights too far to reach. The next day it would be biting, frigid, painful on the skin like a first-degree burn and tormenting for the body since no matter how many layers you hid under, you still shivered. And, of course, the following day, the breeze would be humid, electric, clammy on the skin, and irritating to the person trying to sleep without a fan or an air conditioner.

I hated the wind for being so fickle, but I hated it more for its stubbornness.

Another season had passed, and instead of lounging around, I decided to take a walk. It was for health purposes, to keep my heart beating, and to keep my mind out of dark thoughts— lonely thoughts.

The wind was brutal and violent. It seemed that I was wandering into an ensuing storm. I remembered the days I used to soar high above hurricanes and typhoons, escaping their wrath and destruction. I always had a way of avoiding them and continued my trajectory across the cerulean skies undisturbed. I soared in comfort, without conflict. I soared with certainty and skill. It was only when my wings grew too big for me to carry did I begin to feel the temper and stubbornness of the wind.

The wind buffeted my body, tugging me, shoving me. I was jerked here and pulled there. I was pushed down and hurled up. I fought against the wind, rivaled its temper with my very own, but the more I resisted, the more I was pushed around. The wind taunted me as it reminded me of how powerless I was in its grasp. I felt mocked, and my pride hurt. After all, I was always above the wind, above its angry storms and destructive conflicts. I felt I was put in my place, though I knew I belonged in the clear altitudes beyond.

Then the turbulence stopped. At the time, I was too young to understand what the eye of a hurricane meant. It was a brief moment of repose and tranquility, a much-needed interval, before being propelled back into the wrath of the beast. I thought it was over. I thought I could flap my wings past the silver lining of the clouds to meet the sun's golden rays against a canvas of crystal azure. I attempted it as soon as the eye of the hurricane passed me, and I was immediately snatched away from freedom to be tossed about once again. It was then that I thought the winds to be temperamental and cruel. You just never knew what to expect from them.

Looking back on it now, I never truly hated the wind. I was simply a child angry at someone older and wiser, telling me to do something for my own good. At the end of it all, the clouds parted, the sun shone, and I found myself flying over a new sky, a new world. I had always flown in the same place, always soaring high, always reaching and reaching beyond the tallest height. I had never truly soared, never truly flown, like the wind that moved from here to there, one place to the next.

I realized now it wasn't important how high a bird could fly but how far their wings could take them. What use was a bird if it couldn't reach its destination? What use were wings if they were made to soar up and not soar away?

I continued my way down my forest path, to the howling winds and bending trees, beneath a shroud of nimbus clouds, hoping I could be lifted from my feet and be hurled by the wind, wanting not to reach heights unattainable but wishing to be propelled to a world of mystery and delight.

Last summer, I dreamed of the sky. Yesterday, I dreamed of flying high. Today, I followed the wind.

You're On Your Own

Khushi Mahla

I went to the beach

And sat on my favourite bench.

I loved this bench because it was covered with

A shady tree with pink flowers and an ocean view.

It had a flower shop and bookstore in front of it.

I loved that

Because whenever I look at a flower shop now,

I remember Lily from my favourite book,

It ends with us.

It gives me hope.

Someone will unknowingly send me

Flowers.

Maybe.

19 years passed

And no one did.

But Lily gave me strength.

I loved to watch the bookstore in front of me,

People flipping pages,

People buying tons of books,
People picking flowers
For their loved ones.
I loved to watch all this.
I could never get rid of this
Mesmerizing view.
I hoped someone would
Unknowingly send me
Books and flowers
But no one did.
And one fine day,
I started walking from the bench.
I picked yellow sunflowers,
My favourite,
Because they gave me strength.
And I bought them for myself.
I went to the bookstore and
Bought around 5-6 books,
The ones on my wishlist
From a long time ago.
I realised, why wait for someone
When I can do all this for myself?
Maybe Lily, sunflowers, and books
Inspired strength in me
To face reality.

Alter Ego

BB

I want to be seen

I want to be heard

I want to be well-read with books on my shelf I bought as a
teenager and never finished

I want to file my grandparents' pictures to remember the day they
fought on their way to their honeymoon

I want to be dressed in chic and plaid skirts, my bare skin showing
without the fear of strange hands

I want to speak aloud with not just words but with angst,
emotion—slam the poetry I wrote

I want to learn new words, words that I find magical, philosophical,
historical—words with power and voice

I want to sink into the arms of that fictional boy who I thought was
real when I dreamt of him

I want to find him, find him in someone

I want to reach out to people's hands to save myself from falls
rushing down my throat and up my neck

I want to be intelligent, to speak hours of paragraphs to
satisfy myself

I want to learn physics and math and how the earth moves

I want to watch classic movies to imagine myself in a new scenario
every day, to find an escape

I want to be the male lead, to walk like iron and cry my eyes
when I see my mum

hell, I want to be forrest gump

I want to fit in the party of people where stories are made and
destroyed

where love is found and lost

where hands are held at night

beneath the blanket

fit in where glasses are poured over intellect and not ice

fit in the world of dark academia and poetry

fit into my mother's jeans

I want to love the freckle on his finger if he allows me

I want to be as pretty as Rose in Titanic

I want to be chosen, to be kept forever in a small, fragile case of
glass somewhere like a rose in

the museum of their eyes

I want to be held tight with everything he owns, from palms,
eyes, jackets, and words

I want to smell like a candle from medieval times with lavender
essence and innocence

I want to be brave like the people battling puzzles in their minds

My Friends Don't Know I'm Special

Leah Legan

I slide my hands underneath the child's arms. As gently as I can, I lift him. The little boy offers no complaint. With my help, he rises placidly onto his stone-colored rental skates. His squarish face, soft with the innocence only a four-year-old possesses, is as smooth as the surface of the rink. The little boy stands on his own for a mere moment before his smooth expression melts. I look around nervously— what other coaches are nearby? I ready myself, but he doesn't cry.

He raises his doll-like fingers, sheathed in woolly black gloves, to his pale face. Then he laughs. Minuscule shards of ice coat his fingers; in such a number, they may as well be snow. He brings his hands to his side. I shift my weight, rocking farther onto my toe picks.

"Thomas, "I say, "we need to keep going."

He looks directly into my eyes with his small face.

"Cold," he squeaks. He begins to move his hands, playing with the snow on his dark gloves and the sensation of ice on his tiny body. His mouth has shaped itself into a wild smile; I can see each of his teeth.

Taking this moment from him would be cruel, so I wait. My eyes never leave his fingers. They move as if the boy was given the power of a god, only to try and hold it in his hands.

Finally, I urge Thomas onwards and focus on the air stinging my cheeks instead of my own hands.

*****

I was in a circus. It was school produced, perfectly manufactured. We were so excited. Many of the children rejoiced at the chance to skip class. I mostly loved watching the members of the show. My favorite was the acrobats. It was a dream born in kindergarten, a pint-size idea I knew I needed to achieve, if only for the heck of it.

Things were different when you were smaller, with a Kit Kittredge bob and the confidence to match.

There were a few videos of my hand flapping. I remember once, in elementary school, my mom showed me one of someone else. This alien girl waved her hands. I asked questions once I began to notice the lack of other kids who moved their hands as I did.

"It's how you were born," my mom explained, the same as she would to Davis years later.

My flapping could be seen in videos taken before I became conscious of my otherness.

Such was the second-grade circus. I was standing slightly backstage, almost bouncing and rocking my whole body. It was nearly time for our act. Tied around my waist was a sash the colour of Pepto Bismol. Despite the colour, it was the sash I had wanted since I first saw the acrobats perform. The fabric stood stark against my white shirt and leggings. Someone gathered my blonde hair into a ponytail perfect for performing whirlwinds of cartwheels and somersaults.

I was a perfect child: a sweet acrobat, a second grader. But I was grinning wide, and I was twitching.

I paused, stretched my lips further, and did this again. Many people saw the recording of the circus— many people were there to see its premiere.

What did they think of me?

My own oblivion now makes me sick.

I want to laugh at that little girl and her naivete to prevent me from turning my thoughts to darker things. In the video, she links arms with her smiling classmates, who couldn't understand her hands. I suppose they were still young. It didn't matter yet. One day, though, those girls grew up.

People smile at children with "quirks." There is an understanding that they will grow out of these behaviors. But if they do not?

Then they are named special or broken. They must find a solution or face the bless-your-heart glances, the arched brows, and the double looks.

No god fixed me. I fixed myself, though I have begun to wonder if I shattered something in the process.

*****

Much like Thomas, my brother is young. Younger than me, I correct myself. Davis is a 10-year-old fifth grader— six years older than my learn-to-skate student. He's grown-up enough to stand on a field armored by Dick's Sporting Goods version of bubble wrap. Through a mixture of voices, leaves in the wind, and cars, there's the chirp of a whistle.

Davis runs. At this moment, I am sure he is fantastic. He is Tom Brady— though on the defensive line— or a hero from Marvel's Avengers. Perhaps that is an accurate line of thinking because I see him fluster the quarterback into fumbling a pass.

After the play, he brings his hands to his chest, then swings them against each other. Though I'm far away, I have seen him do it enough that I know his teammates hear the sound of wings.

I have lost count of the treacherous number of moments I've seen him do this.

Yet, I am sure it is many. His hands have danced since he was Thomas' age—maybe even before. But somehow, he's managed to hold onto his craving for sensation, even managed to sustain his enjoyment. The reason behind this eludes me, as does the number of times I have bothered him about it.

One day, Davis mentioned an incident to my mother and me. Another boy laughed at how his hands oscillated while my sweet brother talked about sports. He had defended himself, but I could sense an underlying shroud of upset.

"Why can't you just stop?" I had asked.

I hated myself the next moment. The question wasn't kind nor fair—I knew this. I also knew that Davis did have friends, even a budding girlfriend. He hadn't been ostracized for something he did not choose to deal with.

It wasn't that I wanted him to feel as I did, to sit on his fingers at the slightest tinge of excitement. I hope I am a better sister than that. Yet, I am agitated. Perhaps it is the sticking feeling that his luck won't last. Children are more like ravens than dolls. They are calculating and cruel. They have keen eyesight—so perceptive that it is easy for them to spot the *unbelonging*.

Memories

Marissa Wilfahrt

Memories, painful as they are, we cope with them.

The power they hold over our spirituality, our emotions, our actions—

The beauty of a memory's impulsivity.

We may see one thing on life's road that serves as a memory's key, but a memory may have hundreds of keys,

Reminders of places and time, bliss and anguish, good judgment triumphing over evil, and evil winning one of the war's battles.

Just as battles lead to the war's outcome, aspects of circumstance build a memory.

Why didn't your head close that memory's branch?

What is it that makes that memory so dire to your survival?

Perhaps it is holding the hand of a loved one.

Perhaps it is being taught a lesson that shaped your future.

Or perhaps it is grasping as tightly to a piece of your past as you can.

Hold on.

Control these memories.

Use them to your life's advantage, for all memories are, at one point or another, inevitably forgotten.

Autumn Tears

Olympuz

As the leaves turn brown,
As they fall down,
The heart gets colder, darker.

I can see your frown.
You've dropped your crown.
You can't be sober.

Through all of these years,
All your autumn tears
Have ruined your October.

But now that you're here
We can disappear
Your suffering will finally be over.

The Hope I Want Found

Ashlesha Misra

The frost sets in

As the dew wets the grounds,

New hope is found as the coldness is left out.

The beauty of the past in the future unfound,

But where are you hope, the one I want found?

The heart shatters as the mind restores,

The will weakens as the shadows overgrow,

It's life that gives us so much joy, and yet it is life that kills us inside.

Where are you hope, the one I want found?

Time may pass,

Age might grow, yet childlike we are inside,

With time that never flows.

In unmarked lands, we rest, and in unmarked graves, our hearts lie.

We are broken

But smile to hide what's inside.

Where are you hope, the one I want found?

Listen well to the grass and snow.

I know my heart is no more.

As the seasons change and the years pass,

My heart will someday, maybe one day,

Know,

Know that it was loved, know that if it were mourned,
know that it shall forever be known.

I have found the hope I wanted found.

Love, Emilie

Claire Casapao

11th November 2022

Amelia, I haven't been doing well lately. It's nearly midnight. Ellen had an asthma attack, and she's hospitalized at the moment. I'm currently alone at home. I wonder if you've ever felt as alone as I do now.

I can see your bright, expressive eyes, perfect smile, and gorgeous black hair everywhere. You're still playing the flute in my mind's eye, and I can still hear the gentle melody of 'City of Stars' whenever I touch the keys of my piano.

Love,
Emilie

*****

1st December 2022

Amelia, it's raining outside. Ellen's joined you at the pearly gate. The homework on my table is unfinished, and I remember how I used to listen to your voice as you presented speeches and won debates.

We never knew each other. All I did was watch your perfect life in pictures as it moved to a close. I remember the surge of jealousy I felt every time I saw your awards. I remember the motivation to do better running through my veins.

I wanted to be you. No, I wanted to be *better* than you. You had that one thing I could never have—perfection. I spent hours practicing Fur Elise and La Campanella on the piano just so I could tell people I had mastered those pieces. I spent hours poring over my history project because I was so sure you would do better.

I became nicer; I curbed my sharp tongue; I tried everything I could to be a better leader. I did everything in my power to become as perfect as you. It worked, Amelia. My best friends believe I'm perfect. The entire school believes I'm perfect.

Just as they believed that about you. We never knew that you were under so much pressure. So much pressure that you decided to take your own life.

If only I could go back in time and choose not to start competing with you, we could've been the best of friends.

But I still want to thank you, Amelia. If it weren't for you, I wouldn't be where I am today.

Love,

Emilie

*****

27th January 2023

Amelia, I've always wondered how your family coped with your death. Mine is having a hard time with Ellen's passing. Your socialite parents are still doing charity work, smiling at orphans, looking like they never lost you. Did they care about you? Did they love you as much as your friends did?

I had tea with your parents yesterday. I couldn't find a single picture of you in their house. I wanted to see those kind eyes and that sweet smile in a physical photograph. Oh, Amelia, I miss you. We only passed each other in the halls, but the entire school felt your loss. People did care about you, Amy.

Isn't that what your closest friends called you? *Amy?*

I can feel the shadow of death everywhere. At home, my parents are still crying over Ellen. I miss Ellen. I also miss how you challenged me to be better than I already was. You never knew that you inspired so many people, including me.

Thank you so much, Amy. I hope I can see you and Ellen again.

Love,

Emilie

coming of age
Czarina Datiles

i know nothing

except that two and two make four,

kindness

is giving,

never asking more,

and that respect is paid tribute

to those who are wise and old.

i know nothing

except that pageant smiles

get gold stars on behavior boards,

grades determine

who you are,

and children are mean

when they're taught to be so.

i know nothing

except that friendly dispositions

get you friends— even boys,

a compliment

brightens a stranger's world,

and that it's better to be agreeable

than honest when you're a girl.

i knew nothing then,

and i still know nothing now,

but what they teach you in grade school

about how Columbus sailed the ocean blue

in 1492

and how perfect scores

lead to rose gold success

makes you a fool,

a wanderer,

a gullible idiot with a beautiful smile

ready to be eaten alive

in a world so cruel.

i know now that

one plus one makes three,

and that doesn't always make

people happy.

kindness

is authenticity

and doesn't mean it can't be paid.

respect is earned and not given,

despite what the old folks say.

i know now that

pageant smiles only go so far

when the runway ends,

and facades don't really count for friends.

grades do determine who you are

so long as you allow them to do so.

children are just as naive and impressionable

as I am

and express what they can't at home.

i know now

that friendly dispositions

do get the boys

and that too pretty of a smile,

too careless of a glance,

make them think you want something more.

a single compliment

can get you in a stranger's bed,

and when you're too agreeable,

too compliant, too amenable,

you find yourself on the witness stand

or in a psych ward for wishing you were dead.

better to be charming than honest in a world

where privilege rules.

Adulthood is nearing,
yet I've learned so few
of the world, I've been forced to
endure and to exist,
taking my shot without a single miss
because I am still a child
in a room full of Grown-ups,
still wishing to be naive,
to never Grow Up.

All the Ash Still Left

Pia

I want my spirit back.

I even miss the rage I once felt.

The fire is better than the cold, but now,

is void of indignation and not ignited.

I think,

"If only Prometheus could tell me his secrets."

No one stole it from me, but perhaps,

that's the worst part.

I grew older, and somewhere between 13 and 17,

I watched it slip through my fingers—

handfuls of ash,

getting lost in flurries of wind.

A fire gone out,

and a sorrow, clinging fog.

What is left? What still grows in winter?

Surely nothing.

Not after I salted the earth with what (few) ashes

of my fire

I had left.

Hunger

Marissa Wilfahrt

An empty human

Why does it attract us so?

Life revolving around its necessity for consumption

As we wonder what stems humanity's contempt for mortality

When the answer lies on the empty plate on our chest

Begging us to fill its space with the finite gratitude of materialism

Pleading for us to alleviate the dense ache of hunger inside

The craving for flavor and for, spice and for sweet,

But the one who leaves his plate empty through the youth of his years

Will be the one whose exodus from mortality will be made comfortable by the fullness of his plate

For his insides are no longer empty, and his mind's imploring has ceased

The full plate bows closer and closer under his feet as he rises

In the realization that he must leave his plate behind

The Sun, The Sand, and The Sea

Kashish Lewis

i used to be afraid
of going back home
with my long hair full of sand
pockets filled with seashells
and a car that needed a day
of water - shampoo - water

i used to be annoyed
when I lost my purple flip flops
to the sun, the sand, and the sea
when my lucky yellow tank top
had stains of ketchup
from the neatly done picnic spread
and the ring I wore
floated away with the waves

but now
as i come here by the waters again
i promise to keep an open mind

and just as i let it all go

surrendering myself to the breeze

it sways me in its arms

like a crying baby

that needs to be soothed

the sea whispers beautiful love notes to me written on tiny grains of
sand

that stick to my calves

as the wave steals all my pain

from beneath my feet

i let loose

and the rhythm

sits on my lips

i take a deep breath

and let it all happen to me

the sun

the sand

and the sea

finally

I feel free

Glaciers of Gorgeousness

Rhythmi Rosa

I had to be a swan in my sea of life
When I was swarmed by the spring of weeds.
This strengthened my willpower to soar high
With sharp swords of trust and dreams.

Spillage of tears during the dark times
Showered luminous sparkles in my sight.
Our eyes will be gifted with glaciers of gorgeousness
For each teardrop unheard by the world.

Centuries roll with the strength of each second
With the same clock in all walks of life.
Let's spread our butterfly wings into the aerial wonders
From our caged pupas of silence and pessimism.

American Dream

Marissa Wilfahrt

In my sophomore year of high school, I realized I wanted to join the Navy. I wanted to be constantly surrounded by people who would motivate me to be the best and bravest person I could be in an environment that fostered thriving military life. When people first asked me why I wanted to join the Navy and how I could be so sure of a decision at such a young age, the only answer I could give them was to try to describe the emotional and physical pull I felt for that career path. That feeling was something I had never felt before and something that I hadn't understood for a long time. All I knew was that I had to grasp that mysterious and raw passion because if I let it free or came up for air for a moment, it might slip out of my hands. Something in my heart constantly told me I couldn't let that happen.

Slowly, I began to understand this powerful feeling inside me, which blossomed every time I heard anything about the military or saw one of its members. By the mere indication of their apparel, these members already had my utmost respect and admiration, alongside all others who looked up to them.

My grandfather and grandmother were two people that I always looked up to my whole life. My grandfather landed on the USS Midway during the Korean War and continued to serve in the Navy for years. Once he retired to a new job piloting for American Airlines, he met his future wife and my future grandmother, his flight attendant. I thought that that feeling pushing me toward the Navy was because of my grandfather, as he passed away from Alzheimer's disease in my freshman year of high school. I was upset that somebody who did so much good and provided so much light in the lives of those around him was doomed to a fate that none of us could prevent, especially since he'd been putting his life on the line for others his whole life. One of those "others" was not supposed to be Alzheimer's. The same undeniable selflessness had always been present in my grandmother's actions that were compensated for by stage IV pancreatic cancer when my siblings and I were very little.

But, as I met more and more military members and people who needed my help or defense, I realized that the feeling I cherished did not stem from my grandfather or grandmother; it stemmed from my compelling desire to help people like them. I couldn't stop their lives from being taken away by cancer or Alzheimer's disease, but if I could spend the rest of my life helping people whose lives I could impact and improve, I decided that would be my way of making a difference in the world, just as they did.

Now, I am learning from my cousin, who is graduating from NROTC (Naval Reserve Officers Training Corps) at Tufts University and has always inspired me and taught me about what it means to be in the Navy. It is the compassion and necessity to put others first that has driven me to the reality that the only thing that could possibly satisfy my aspirations for life is serving my country and giving my life up for others.

On Father's Day in the summer of sophomore year, we visited the Midway to see where my grandfather landed his F-51 fighter jet and where he bunked in his service during the Korean War. The moment we arrived in full sight of the massive carrier, getting closer to it with each step, that special feeling multiplied by a hundred until I thought my heart might burst. My eyes began to tear up as I stared at every angle of the USS Midway, and I knew that joining the Navy was my life's calling. At that moment, I could also pinpoint what that feeling was for the past couple of years. It was a buildup of every war story I'd ever heard; of innocent people paying with their lives for circumstances that were not their fault nor responsibility; and of the most courageous people that would put their lives on the line for the preservation of the right to pursue the American dream. It was the combination of every memory I had speaking with members of the military, all of whom never ceased to stun me with their proud fortitude and pure dedication toward others. All of these memories, emotions, and sweat shed over the years in pursuit of the feeling finally came together in a glorious understanding and assurance that I was going to be a part of that family; I was to don the camouflage uniform of a person dedicating their life to serving the greater good. And I never looked back. Sure, the logistics came shortly afterward, but nothing could make me more motivated and focused than reminding myself that these were all pieces of a puzzle.

Although I do not have all the pieces to this puzzle quite yet, I know that they will all ultimately come together to make my variation of the American dream come true— becoming a member of the United States Navy.

pulling teeth

Mia Grace Davis

when you were younger, you hooked a string around a tooth
and pulled, slamming the door to fish it out. from your gaping

mouth it popped, the first of many to detach from its snug
pocket. you burrowed your earnings beneath your fleece pillow,

a talisman of growth. no longer were you the child
they claimed you to be, with plush cheeks and eyes

teeming with innocence. no longer would your feet carelessly leap across hopscotch squares, stumbling on fractured concrete,

scraping unblemished flesh. no longer would you shove a ring pop
into your mouth like a pacifier as your eyes followed Tom and
Jerry's

every move. no, you were more than happy to leave

this simple life behind. from the moment the tooth

and you cleaved from each other, you could not be the same.

for although you lost part of yourself, you gained maturity

far before the universe intended. little did you know

you would yearn for the return of blissful ignorance

years later. little did you know you would continue pulling teeth,

just not those in the mouth.

Aqua Regia

Anannya Tiwary

How it melts the gold
And makes it perish,
Like our old self does
Once we mature.

Bubbling thoughts,
Pondering waters,
The skin realizes
It is not the same anymore.

It has gone through scratches and bled
When we worked,
It has cried sweat
When we struggled.

When we discover
Most of those around us
Are snakes in disguise,

When we forgive those
Who poisoned us
With bladed nightshades,

When we are no longer bothered
About what people say,
Even if they are close ones,
It doesn't feel toxic anymore.

Sleepless nights,
Mind drowned in wonders,
Worries about the future,
At some point, we realise
What we have become
And mature.

Grown

Marissa Wilfahrt

I look down at this new body—

The long limbs, muscular build, and long brown hair
have chosen my age.

I walk outside on my bare feet with my hair thrown in
a messy bun as I wonder,

When did the world grow so small?

Then I remember as I cling to my younger years,

Oh, my dear,

Take a step forward.

That step forward was the key to unlocking the world,
to unlock its potential.

I let down my long hair, stretched my long limbs, and turned
with a renewed sight upon the world.

Life hadn't gotten smaller.

It had grown so slowly and so carefully over the years as to
ambush me with its vivacity.

I turn to see the color, the prospect, the people around me.

Oh, the people.

Such confident spirits, strutting with the wisdom of their years,
some well beyond.

The language, the apparel, even the scent each exudes—all testaments to their life's advance.

The long hair and limbs alike, the glowing skin with a few scars from the downs of life, the mature posture.

The wide smile hiding the pain a thousand more years could not cure.

But then, from behind their bodies runs a miniature version of each of them, alive with the newness of their world, a world so seemingly small because they have not experienced it yet.

With their short hair, stout arms and legs, the smiles with nothing yet to hide, with nothing waiting to be uncovered, their eyes not yet clouded with the tears of fatigue or vigor, heartbreak or burning passion, hardship or sheer perseverance used to overcome—

I was them.

17 Years

Kelly Keyes

I thought I'd turn into a sweet butterfly,
Eclose from my chrysalis, let my wings dry.
Meconium would spread throughout my frail frame,
Then I'd spread out my wings and flit up to the sky.

I'd grace the whole world like a soft lullaby,
Bless the curious stares of young passersby.
I'd dazzle with beauty, burn bright like a flame,
Lasting only two weeks before leaving to die.

But instead, I came out like a plan gone awry,
Emerged from the ground in the heat of July.
After 17 years, I shed my shell and my name,
And I shattered the air with a horrible cry.

As the time to go on with my life was now nigh,
I examined my form with a red compound eye.
Turns out, cicadas have wings all the same,
So who cares if I'm pretty; I'm still soaring high.

Meet the Co-Authors

Khushi Mahla

Khushi Mahla is an ardent reader but still doesn't think she reads enough to be called one. Living in a fantasy world, she writes to make herself happy, making her words fly to you. The only inspiration she looks to is Sunflower. Always patient, she is trying to fit in and survive in this bustling world.

Aarushi Agarwal

Aarushi Agarwal is a budding poet and writer. Her poetry transcribes raw emotions felt in real moments. With a belief in the profound balance that underlies all things in life, Aarushi hopes everyone embraces the beauty in light and shadows. She believes poetry to be the language of emotions, perfectly capturing moments in life, both real and imaginary, through words and phrases. She has participated in multiple poetry competitions and is carving her path as a poet with her first poetry publication.

Olympuz

Olympuz is the pen name of Gabriel Elias Josende, a Brazilian writer and poet with three published poetry books.

Binta Elsa Biju

Binta Elsa Biju is a postgraduate in English Language and Literature who is an ardent admirer of art and literature. She is a passionate soul, eagerly wishing to advocate for fruitful thoughts and actions. She is fond of reading, writing poems, and exploring novel areas of literature that grab her attention.

Divvya Gupta

Divvya Gupta, a Chartered Accountant by profession, is driven by her keen interest in weaving words in a rhythmic style that can convey vital messages to society. She strives to make her words so impactful that they lead to the creation of a better person, society, and a far better world.

Ashlesha Misra

Sometimes, the world is out to get us. Sometimes the world feels like it's standing against us. But, if you look deep inside your heart, you will find an Ashlesha in you. You will find a star in your heart.

Anannya Tiwary

Anannya Tiwary is a 17-year-old poet and nature enthusiast. She has won prizes in numerous poetry competitions, including the Kavyanjali poetry competition held by the Wildlife Institute of India. She is an avid reader and is fond of playing piano in her leisure time.

Pawan Kumar

Pawan Kumar is an accomplished Senior Business Analyst in the aviation sector and has been with a prestigious multinational travel corporation for the entirety of his professional career. A law and science graduate with a natural gift for storytelling, his words have the power to evoke

emotions, ignite imaginations, and provoke thought. Pawan likes to read, write, and explore new genres of life. His interests vary from food to business to technology and nature. To stay updated on Pawan's literary and travel adventures, follow him on Instagram at @__pawankumar.

Abigail Alcala

Abigail Alcala is of Mexican descent and was raised in San Diego. Since she was very young, she has always written her own books and has always loved to write. Writing has helped her find who she is today and express her emotions differently. She is very close to her family and tells them everything that comes to her mind. She finds peace in butterflies and resonates with their metamorphosis.

BB

Bhakti is a psychology major and a psycho in nature. She is very creative with her words and how she pours out her entangled mind on paper as a single thread. Bhakti loves watching true crime documentaries, which do not match her empathetic nature. Her quirkiness stems from how basic she  can be, and her ironically stupid jokes will bring out a disgusted chuckle from people around her. She is the personification of her poems and art, without which she would not feel alive or human.

Jasmeen Bagga

 Jasmeen Bagga is a 19-year-old medical student and author hailing from the city of Ludhiana, Punjab. With two published books on Wattpad and a recent co-authorship of an anthology, she has already made her way into the literary world. As a new university student, she is navigating the challenges of balancing her studies with everyday tasks such as laundry and dishes. She couldn't have written this piece without the unwavering support of a friendly stranger, who soon became a good friend to her and encouraged her to confront her fear of writing again. She dreams of publishing her own book someday, one that captures her unique perspective on the world.

Claire Casapao

Claire Casapao is an ambitious high school student with aspirations of graduating at the top of her class. Despite her grand academic plans, she still makes time for her not-so-secret passion: writing.

Jothika Pandiarajan

Jothika Pandiarajan is a BNYS 1st Year student at JSS Institute of Naturopathy and Yogic Science College in Coimbatore, Tamil Nadu, India. She's an enthusiastic and optimistic person. She loves writing and writes for newspapers and journals as a hobby. To her, writing is like therapy, where she finds cures for everything. Her passion for writing started with discouragement from others. She believes life is a one-time journey where we must enjoy every aspect.

Pavika Pandey

Pavika Pandey, also known as Heer, is a 19-year-old writer from Haryana, India. She first started writing when she was 13. She has been reading various novels since she was very young and is fascinated with the art of expressing emotions through different words. Heer has also been an international-level kathak performer since she was six years old. Her poems are featured in PoetrySoup, and she has won the "Latashree Poetry Competition." She was formerly a student at Delhi Public School and is pursuing her medical career.

Mia Grace Davis

Mia Grace Davis is a writer and editor at Stanford University. She has pieces featured/forthcoming in *Gone Lawn*, *The Tusculum Review*, and *Ice Lolly Review*, among others. She is a 2023 National YoungArts Finalist in Writing (Spoken Word) and a U.S. Presidential Scholars in the Arts Semi-finalist. Visit her at miagracedavis.com.

Kashish Lewis

Kashish Lewis, author of You Me and Love, is a poet from Bangalore, Karnataka. She describes herself as a hopeless romantic who buries herself between the pages of a spine-chilling story or mystical poetry for comfort. Her love for travel and events— and her urge to always try something new— makes her an entrepreneur. She is the founder of Inkfeathers Stage & PrepEdge.

Sanaa Shaikh

A nerd and an amateur writer packed in one, Sanaa is a sixteen-year-old girl with big dreams and an unwavering will to fulfil them. She is a student in Class XI at Delhi Public School, Gurgaon. Sanaa is an aspiring psychologist. Nothing brings her greater joy than a freshly brewed cup of coffee and a book to curl up with. "Go big or go home" are words she lives by.

Kelly Keyes

Kelly Keyes is a poet from Portland, Oregon. Her work combines the natural beauty of the world with her own journey of self-discovery. In her free time, Kelly enjoys going on walks, playing open-world games, and people-watching.

Rhythmi Rosa

Rhythmi Rosa S is a poet from India. She loves writing poetry, articles, quotes, and short stories in English and Tamil. She won first place in two poetry competitions during her college days. Her literary creations are mostly based on motivational, nature-based, fantasy, and meaningful themes.

Marissa Wilfahrt

Marissa Wilfahrt is a rising student, athlete, writer, published illustrator, and armed forces member. She is the youngest of three children and enjoys music, sports, public speaking, reading, travelling, and spending time with loved ones. She loves to connect with others through her writing and lets the

power of emotion, experience, and circumstance drive her words. Marissa is confident in every person's ability to express on paper what cannot be said aloud and to use their unique language to inspire and reach into the hearts and minds of others.

Saraswathy

Saraswathy is a working mother who likes to listen to music, read, travel, and chill at home.

Pia

Pia grew up in Southern California. She likes to read and sketch in her free time and loves the outdoors. She currently has plans to major in English.

We love creating beautiful books for you!

Come be a part of our ever-growing community of authors. Grow, write, and publish with us!

Scan here to explore books, authors and more

Connect with us on socials. We'd love to hear from you!

    Inkfeathers Publishing